Snow Daze

The Snowberry Series Book 1

Katie Mettner

ISBN-10 : 1493732145
ISBN-13 : 978-1493732142

Cover design by: Carrie Butler
Printed in the United States of America

Dear Reader,

When you first meet Snow, I'm sure you'll be surprised when you're introduced to MAC, the highly complicated wheelchair she uses in this story. Most readers think it's not real. This is fiction, after all, right? The truth is, there is a real prototype of this chair undergoing tests and trials as we speak. It started in a guy's garage made from a lawn chair, a motor and wheels, to a fully functional voice recognition wheelchair. The technology was already at our fingertips to bring a chair like this to the market, so it makes sense this is the next step. I hope one day I can sit in one of these chairs and say, "Forward, hands" and be able to hold hands with my husband while my wheelchair does the work. I want you to know that I strive to make my stories as realistic as I can because you, the reader, deserve that. While the chair is not on the market yet, I enjoyed writing a story based on the idea that one day it will be, and it will change the lives of so many people!

Be well,

Katie

For My Dully Alexander

Chapter One

There came a telltale drop, and then a sudden jerk, that rocked me backward into the side of the elevator. Great, just great, the meeting starts in ten minutes, and the elevator is stuck again. I grabbed the phone inside the door of the elevator panel and waited impatiently for the operator. When she picked up, I wanted to yell, but my midwestern upbringing had me making pleasantries first.

"Hi, Jo, how are you doing today?" I asked, giving myself a mental head slap. The voice on the other end of the line was lilting with laughter when she answered.

"I'm doing just fine, Dr. Snow, but you seem to be stuck again." She chuckled as I heard the keys clicking on her keyboard.

"Again is the key word here, Jo. For the love of Sam, when are they going to get this thing fixed?" I asked, the exasperation clear in my voice.

"You know the answer to that, Dr. Snow!"

"Never!" We both said in unison, and we laughed like two schoolgirls in the schoolyard.

"I have notified Bernie you're stuck, again, and he's on his way. I'll let Dr. Fleetwood know you will be a little late, and promise to have a coffee waiting when you roll off that elevator. Anything else, Dr. Snow?" she asked, trying not to laugh.

I sighed. "Nope, that should do it, Jo. Is it sad we have this down to a science?"

"We probably shouldn't delve too deep into that statement. Enjoy your break!"

I laughed, shook my head, and hung up the phone. "I should have taken the stairs."

The words were barely out of my mouth, and I heard a snort behind me. I turned, and it was then I remembered I wasn't alone. The stranger in the elevator with me had his hands braced on the rails and was backed into the corner. He was going for nonchalant, but he was failing. His expression screamed fear.

I took in the man before me. He was five-six if he was that, and what looked to be a well-defined buck seventy-five. He was dressed sharply in a polo shirt and black jeans, with a pair of Crocs adorning his feet. I couldn't help but chuckle at the decorative buttons with SpongeBob, Lightning McQueen, and Mickey Mouse, just to name a few. I let my eyes wander back up to his face and made eye contact.

His eyes were unusual, one was light grey, and one was dark green. His hair fell over his eyes in a shaggy appearance of a schoolboy, but when he smiled, it was captivating. It must have been contagious because I found myself smiling, despite the fact we were trapped in an elevator.

"Did you find something I said funny, Mr...." I

paused, waiting for him to fill in the blank.

He leaned forward and stuck out his hand, "Mr. Alexander, but anyone as beautiful as you can call me Dully."

I took his hand and shook it firmly, trying not to roll my eyes at the worst possible pickup line ever. "Nice to meet you, Dully. I'm Snow."

He released my hand and leaned back to grab the rail. "The pleasure is all mine, Snow..." He left the sentence open, waiting for me to fill in the blank.

"Daze. Snow Daze," I answered.

His brow went up, and I lost my fight with the snicker. Living with the name Snow Daze for the last twenty-eight years has been a trial. I doubt anyone has a joke I haven't heard, but people still try.

"What a beautiful name. It fits you," he said simply, and I felt my mouth drop open a little.

"Um, thank you?" I half muttered, running a hand through my hair. I rarely got flustered, but one compliment from him and I couldn't remember my name.

"You're welcome."

I smiled up at him. "So, I suppose this is our meet-cute?"

"Our meet-cute?" he stopped for a moment and then shook his finger at me. "I suppose it is. Two strangers riding the same elevator, one a beautiful woman, the other a good looking, sexy guy, and the elevator abruptly stops, jostling them into each other. Definitely our meet-cute."

"Ha! Sounds like the perfect opening to a Danielle Steel novel," I admitted, laughing.

"Who?" he asked.

I snickered. Only the most popular romance author in history.

I waved my hand. "Nothing. Of course, we weren't jostled into each other," I reminded him.

"Call it creative license." His gaze held mine, his eyes drawing me in. "So, I gather this happens a lot?" He motioned around the small elevator.

I gave him the palms up. "All the time. I think Bernie does it just to make me take a ten-minute break."

"Who is Bernie?" he asked perplexed.

"He's the maintenance man here at Providence. Sweetest guy in the world, but he sure knows how to throw a pickle in my day," I explained.

"A pickle, huh? That makes me wonder why he thinks you need a ten-minute break."

I shrugged. "Probably because he thinks I work too hard. That or he takes joy in making Dr. Fleetwood wait for me. Perhaps it's both. He definitely can't stand Dr. Fleetwood."

"You're a doctor?" he asked, taking in my white coat with a raised brow.

"Of sorts. I'm actually a clinical researcher," I answered, suddenly feeling a little uncomfortable under his gaze.

"Ah, a brainiac!" He flashed his smile again, and I laughed against my will.

"I guess some would say that," I agreed, feeling my phone vibrate in my pocket, but choosing to ignore it. "What brings you to Providence Hospital this fine day, Dully?"

He glanced down at the bag at his feet and then back to me without making eye contact. "Visiting a student. He decided that checking into the hospital was a legitimate reason to skip school."

"You're a teacher?" I asked, and he nodded the affirmative. "Ah, a brainiac!" I smirked, and he tossed his head back and laughed.

"I guess some would say that." He winked, and I felt my face flush instantly. At that moment, the elevator jerked as it started up again and moved us upward to the next floor. "Looks like Bernie decided your break is over." Dully smiled, grabbing his bag and sliding it over his shoulder.

"Looks like it," I parroted, tapping my fingers on my leg. I hated to admit to myself I was a little sad the doors would be opening, and we'd part ways. I was enjoying Dully's company, which took me very much by surprise.

The door dinged and slid open to reveal the fourth floor of the hospital. Dully held the door open as I exited the elevator. "Thanks for the meet-cute," Dully said from behind me. "Maybe someday we can write the next chapter?" I turned my chair and he was stepping out of the elevator as the doors close behind him.

I tried to think of a way to avoid answering his question. "Is this your stop?" I asked, knowing full well it wasn't since only research was housed on the fourth floor.

He shook his head and pointed to the door with the stair sign on it. "Nope, but I think I'll take the stairs." He winked again and gave me a small wave before pulling open the heavy steel door and disappearing from sight.

Chapter Two

Dully

The steel door closed behind me and I dropped my bag, leaned against the wall, and took several deep breaths. There was nothing worse, in my opinion, than getting stuck in an elevator. It certainly wasn't very manly to freak out or vomit, but that's what I felt like doing. It was especially unmanly when a woman as hot as Snow was staring at you, wondering if you were going to freak out or vomit.

I closed my eyes and let my heartbeat settle down before I picked my bag back up and started up the stairs. I couldn't get my mind off the woman in the elevator. Snow Daze. It might be a unique name, but it fit the most unique woman I had just met. Her hair was snow-white, something I had never seen on anyone younger than seventy. She also had an aura about her that spoke volumes about the things she's been through, and still goes through.

Her beautiful blue eyes glistened when she smiled, and her white lab coat was covering a tiny but curvy body I was struggling not to think too hard about. I paused with one foot on a stair and quirked an eyebrow. "Was that our meet-cute?"

The stairwell remained silent, and I laughed aloud. It was definitely a meet-cute and Snow Daze was definitely a woman I want to know more about. I opened the door to the fifth floor and stepped onto the pediatric unit of Providence Hospital. It was bright and vibrant. The walls held murals of every cartoon character imaginable. There were tanks filled with fish, wagons, a toy room, an activity room, and a quiet reading corner. The low hum of children's voices punctuated by laughter every so often, almost made you forget those same kids were sick. I made my way to the nurse's station, and a young clerk glanced up.

"Can I help you?" she asked, digging through a paper file.

"I hope so. I'm looking for Adam McGregory," I explained.

"Can I see some ID?"

I happily obliged, glad they took the safety of their littlest patients seriously. She inspected my driver's license, then checked a clipboard.

"Of course, Mr. Alexander, you're on the list as an approved visitor." She grabbed a visitor's pass, marked my name and date on it, and handed it over. "He's in room 415. Down the hall to the end room," she informed me smiling, and I thanked her, peeling off the back of the sticker and sticking it to my shirt.

I hitched my bag over my shoulder and made my way down the hallway. I stopped in front of his room and carefully pushed the door open, knocking quietly.

"Come in," a familiar voice said. I stepped into the brightly lit room to see one of my favorite students sitting up in his bed. The window was open to let in some fresh air and sunshine. It might be November in southern Minnesota, but the temperatures were closer to early October. We were enjoying an unexpected late fall, but it wouldn't last long.

"Hi, Adam! We missed you in class again yesterday," I said enthusiastically, setting my bag down.

"Mr. Dully!" Adam exclaimed, happy to see me.

"Hi, Dully, it was nice of you to come," Adam's mother said from where she sat in the recliner next to his bed.

I reached out and patted her shoulder gently, "I miss Adam every day he's not in my class, Ms. McGregory. I thought I'd stop over and see how he's doing. I also brought..." I drew out the sentence, waiting for Adam to answer.

"UNO!" he shouted exuberantly.

"You guessed it, Adam, how do you do that?" I asked, feigning surprise.

"Mr. Dully, you always bring Uno when I'm sick," he pointed out maturely.

"Well, it is your favorite game, Adam and..." I reached into my bag and pulled out a bag of candy.

"Tootsie Rolls!" he said excitedly.

I winked at him. "One now, but the rest you gotta earn." I handed him the bag, so he could pick out his favorite flavor.

I glanced over to see tears in his mother's eyes. The stress of raising Adam alone must be overwhelming sometimes. Born with Down Syndrome, he was often in the hospital because of his heart, and I knew how hard it was for her to juggle all of her responsibilities. Thankfully, she worked at Providence as a nurse. She could work and still be close to Adam when he was sick.

"Why don't you go home and grab a shower and a break, Ms. McGregory? I'll stay with Adam. I've got the whole day free.

She glanced at Adam and then back to me without saying anything.

"It's okay, momma, you deserve a break. I'll be okay with Mr. Dully," Adam assured her.

She kissed his forehead so he wouldn't see her cry. At ten-years-old, he'd already been through more pain than most people twice his age. He was always a trooper and never wanted his mom to worry.

"I know you'll have a lot of fun with Mr. Dully, baby. I'll go home and check on Mr. Monster, and then be back in a few hours," she promised. She fixed his blankets up around his chest, being careful of the drain that snaked from his skin.

"Mr. Monster?" I asked, taking a seat in the chair his mother had just vacated, and digging out the Uno cards.

"You know Mr. Monster! He's my guinea pig," Adam reminded me. I laughed with him then as he launched into a new story about his crazy Mr. Monster.

Snow

I sat listening to Dr. Fleetwood ramble on about something I didn't find compelling enough to listen to. I was still focused on Mr. Dully Alexander, my mystery elevator man. My meet-cute. He was definitely cute, as much as I hated to admit it. As a doctor, I spotted his heterochromia iridum immediately. It was a relatively uncommon autosomal dominant trait that resulted in two different colored irises. As a researcher, I found it fascinating. As a woman, I found it sexy as hell. Admitting that to myself caused a chill to run down my spine. The only men I spent time with were my scientific colleagues, which was on purpose. I didn't need the complications a relationship was sure to bring. Maybe I wasn't being fair to the entire male species by lumping them all into the same category as Vince, but I didn't much care. When Vince left me for someone more *suitable* for his lifestyle, I swore off men for good. For the last three years, that decision had worked just fine for me.

"Snow. Snow." I glanced up at Dr. Fleetwood, who was calling my name.

"Uh, yeah, sorry, Dr. Fleetwood," I answered, trying to recall the last ten minutes of the discussion I'd zoned out on.

"A little distracted this morning, Dr. Daze?" He

smiled, and I let out a breath.

"A little," I admitted. "I do apologize for not giving you my undivided attention. I guess Bernie broke my stride with that elevator break."

"That darn Bernie. You know he's after me, and not you, right?" he asked, folding his hands on the table.

I laughed aloud. "Is that so? Maybe next time he should trap you in the elevator, and let me sit here and drink coffee," I said, taking a sip of my very hot, very sweet, very black coffee.

"That's true, but I don't think Bernie would get nearly as much joy out of it. We can keep it our little secret that we've got his plan figured out. I have a few ideas of ways to get him back. Are you in?" He wiggled his eyebrows evilly. I set my cup down and nodded in the affirmative, giving him a little fist bump.

I rejoined the conversation about flash drives and voice recognition, but my mind was still in that elevator, lost in the mismatched eyes of a guaranteed complication.

It was late, and I was tired, hungry, and sore. I had spent the last three hours showing the research team how the adjustments they had made to the chair had allowed me to do more things at once. That said, after Mac knocked me out of the chair three times, I had to call it a day. There was a glitch in the programming somewhere, and they needed to find it and fix it, or Mac was going to find a new home. MAC stood for Memory Assisted Chair, but the only thing he seemed to be able to remember was how to eject his passenger. I gathered my files and tucked them alongside my leg as I wheeled toward the front entrance of the hospital. I was more than ready for a day off tomorrow, the first in more than a month. The large entry doors slid open as I approached, and the wind blew strong with the loss of vacuum. My files flapped in the wind, and I made a quick grab for them.

"Mac, stop!" I demanded, reaching for the files. I realized too late that the chair had stopped, but I hadn't. The chair tipped toward the ground and put my hands out to catch myself.

"Whoa, cowgirl!" said a voice behind me, and then the chair stopped mid tip. I didn't need to turn to know who it was, and embarrassment started to stain my cheeks pink. He came around the chair and gathered my file folders, straightened the papers, and handed them back with a smile. "Nice to see you again, Dr. Snow. Maybe you need a seatbelt on that bucking bronco."

I accepted the papers but kept my eyes averted, so he wouldn't see the embarrassment on my face. "Thank you, Dully, sorry to bother you."

"No bother at all, Dr. Snow." He smiled and gave me a jaunty salute.

"Really, you can just call me Snow," I insisted,

straightening myself in the chair and tucking the folders behind my back, in hopes of keeping them off the ground.

"Okay, *just call me Snow*, I'm glad we ran into each other again. I've been thinking about you all day," he admitted, glancing at his watch. "If it wasn't so late, I'd ask you to dinner."

I glanced up quickly and right into his mysterious eyes. "Dinner?"

"Yeah, you know, that thing where you sit down, order food, and then put it in your mouth," he explained with a wink.

"Well, well, Mr. Alexander, aren't you a comedian. I know what dinner is. I meant, you know, with me." The last part came out sounding awkward and stupid. I almost smacked myself in the head but thought better of it at the last moment.

"Yes, with you, Snow. Would you give me the honor of joining me tomorrow night?" he asked, holding the strap to his bag nervously.

He was asking me to dinner? Seriously? No. No dinner, no coffee, no anything. Just say no. "I'm off tomorrow, but I usually just drink coffee when I'm alone. It's hard to cook for one, and I hate TV dinners, but you know coffee isn't all it's cracked up to be when it comes to nutrition." Shut up, Snow. Shut up, shut up! What is wrong with you, woman?

"I understand. TV dinners definitely aren't all they're cracked up to be. I was planning a trip to Gallo's. Would you care to join me?" he asked again, and I groaned inwardly. That was not playing fair.

Gallo's made the best pizza in all of southern Minnesota, and it had been far too long since I'd been there. My brain said no, but my stomach said yes.

"I do love Gallo's pizza," I said longingly.

"It's the best pizza this side of Chicago. I love their sun-dried tomato and salami pizza."

My mouth watered. He was a man after my own heart.

"And the beer?" I asked jokingly.

"Totally Naked. The only kind worth drinking," he answered.

I clapped my hands together. "Dinner at Gallo's it is then!" I said in a rush, ignoring the voice in my head telling me I was making a huge mistake.

He laughed heartily and rested his hand on the back of my chair. "I'll pick you up at seven?"

"I probably ought to meet you there." I grimaced, and he shook his head.

"Nope, in my world, a man always picks the lady up for a pizza date."

Now it was a date? Duh, Snow. Why else would he be asking you to dinner?

I cleared my throat before I spoke, so it didn't squeak. "What's your number?" I asked, pulling my phone from my pocket. He rattled it off and I typed it into a text message. I sent him my address, adding, *Don't be late*. His phone dinged, and he grinned when he read the message.

"I'll be there with bells on. See you then." He gave my shoulder a squeeze and waved goodbye, hitching his bag over his shoulder as he walked.

I blew out a breath and grabbed the rims on the chair, spinning them forward. I spent the whole ride home refusing to acknowledge the mistake I had just made.

Chapter Three

I gazed at the ten outfits on the bed for the twentieth time, but they hadn't changed. They all reminded me of something a small-town doctor would wear while making house calls in the 1900s. When did I become Miss Peasant Skirt?

Maybe he likes peasant skirts, a little voice said, and I growled at it.

I rechecked the clock. It was almost five. I certainly didn't have time to go shopping for anything more … stylish. You should have been checking on this at ten o'clock this morning, I scolded myself. Damn Bridget Jones and her diary!

You were too busy pretending it wasn't going to happen by watching movies all day, the little voice said.

"Really, you have got to stop that!" I yelled at the mirror.

About three o'clock, he'd sent a text that said, "*Looking forward to tonight. I thoroughly enjoy your company and find your smile captivating. See you in a few hours!*"

It was a sweet reminder that I had to stop pretending it wasn't happening and start preparing for the date.

I hated to admit I read the text way more times than I needed to. I didn't hear compliments like that one very often. Okay, I never hear them, but that was my own doing. When I swore off guys, I also swore off dating, compliments, and kisses from sexy guys with two different colored eyes.

Considering we had only spent a few moments together, I tried to convince myself it was a cheesy pickup line, but I couldn't. Dully Alexander exuded sincerity, and interestingly enough, I enjoyed his company, too. There was a knock on my front door, and I spun around, my heart pounding. He can't be here already! It's only five o'clock!

"Snow, come on, let me in! I saw your van outside so I know you're in there." I let out a sigh of relief at the voice. It was my bestie, Savannah. She had a key to both doors, in case I ever needed help, but she refused to just walk in unless it was an emergency. She was probably coming to help me get ready. More like she was coming to grill me about the guy who broke my *no dating* streak.

"Coming, Savannah, hold your horses," I shouted, as I made for the door. I pulled it open and was confronted by a massive pile of clothes. Somewhere under there was my friend, so I backed up out of the way and let her through the door with her cumbersome load. She dumped it all on my couch then clapped her hands together excitedly.

"I can't believe you're going on a date!" She smirked while I shut the door and slid the chain back on.

"Geez, Savan, you make me sound like an ogre. And it's not a date, it's just dinner," I informed her. The pile of clothes shifted, and several articles fell to the floor.

"Right, a dinner date!" she squealed, grabbing my hands and jumping up and down. Okay, she's officially lost her mind.

"If I say it's a date, will you chill out?" I asked stoically, and she nodded her head vigorously. "Okay, I'm going on a date tonight with Mr. Alexander."

She wrinkled her nose up as if she had smelled something terrible. "Mr. Alexander? That makes him sound so old! I'm going to call him Mr. Yummy."

I shook my head in exasperation. "How would you know? You've never met him," I laughed with her and led the way back to my bedroom.

She dumped all of the clothes she brought on the bed after pushing my skirts onto the floor. "True, but I checked him out on the school website, and he definitely resides in the yummy category." She glanced around the room and then back to me, dressed in my jeans and old Vikings t-shirt.

"Alright, you need some serious help here." She motioned at the clothes on the bed. "Whatcha gonna wear?" she asked, her Minnesota accent thick.

I giggled in response. "I was just fixin' to decide that," I drawled in a terrible southern accent.

She rolled her eyes at me while she rummaged through her garments. She pulled out several dresses, holding them up to me, one at a time. I wasn't sure what she was looking for, but at that moment I was just happy we both wore the same size. I stared at the choices on the bed, and one caught my eye. I couldn't decide if it was black with red roses or red with black roses, but with a fitted bodice and cap sleeves, it was gorgeous. I pointed to it on the bed. "How about that one?"

She picked it up and hugged it to her. "I love this dress! It's a little small on me, but I think it would fit you perfectly. I'm not sure it will be long enough, though."

I cocked my head. "Long enough for what?" I asked, and her eyes darted to my legs.

"Oh. Wait. What?"

She shrugged uncomfortably. "I know you don't like to show your legs."

"And you know this how?" I asked, confused.

She motioned to the clothes on the floor. "Because you always hide them in peasant skirts and tailored pants."

I almost started in on her about never assuming, but the words died on my lips. She might be right.

"I guess I never thought about that. It wasn't intentional. I guess it just happened over time," I admitted.

Savannah plunked her butt down on the bed. "Does he know?"

I shook my head then shrugged. "I couldn't find a good time in the conversation to bring it up. I mean, he knows about the chair, but he might think it's just for research. I don't know."

I held my hand out for the dress, and she gave it to me. I wheeled to the dressing bench, and slid over onto it, before tugging off my jeans and t-shirt. I slipped the dress over my head, and she came over to help me pull it down under my butt, where it rested a few inches below my knees.

She steepled her fingers and tapped them against her lips. "Oh, I like it! You look … stunning." She held up a finger, and went to my jewelry box, grabbing my ruby necklace and earrings. I put them on, and she rolled the mirror over, so I could see the finished look.

"That'll do, Savan. That'll do," I said quietly.

She moved the mirror aside so she could give me a loving hug.

"It will more than do. He's gonna be blown away! Are you sure you're comfortable with the length?"

I shook my head to the negative. "No, I absolutely am not comfortable with the length, but it's not fair to keep secrets. If he can't take me as I am, then why waste his time and mine." I smacked myself in the forehead with my palm. "Did I just say that?" I whispered.

She laughed and knelt next to me. "Yes, you did, and I agree. I'm also secretly doing a little dance inside that you are ready to join the land of the living again. It's time to make Vince an ugly piece of roadkill in your rearview mirror."

I couldn't contain the laughter that bubbled up from inside me at her suggestion. "I won't be looking in the rearview mirror tonight. He said the man always picks the lady up for a date." I winked, and she threw her arms around me again.

Savannah hugged me tightly while happiness radiated from her. She understood this was a huge step for me, and she was proud of me for taking it. I was proud of myself, too. Scared to death, but proud. Maybe I was ready to join the land of the living again. Perhaps Dully Alexander was my fresh start.

Dully

My feet shuffled nervously on the floor while I waited for the florist to wrap the half dozen roses, and tie them with a bow. Call me old fashioned, but if I'm picking a woman up for a date, I'm bringing flowers. Unfortunately, doubt started to creep in as she readied the bouquet. Maybe I shouldn't have bought the roses. I should have picked up some lovely carnations or daisies. Do roses come off as too serious?

"Um, excuse me. Uh, maybe I should go with some carnations instead," I stuttered, my voice low and unsure.

She smiled and kept wrapping, then carried them over and laid them gently on the counter. "First date?" she asked, and I nodded, swallowing quickly.

"I've been a florist for a long time, and I can tell

you this, no woman in the world thinks roses are too serious. Carnations are nice, but…" she picked the flowers up and handed them to me, "go for the win."

She winked, and I accepted the bouquet, offering her a wave before I left the shop. I lowered myself into my Dodge Magnum and shook out my shoulders. Relax, Dully.

I set the roses on the passenger seat and turned the car over, loving the rumble of the V8 under my feet. It might tank on gas mileage, but it made up for it in fun.

I pulled it into reverse and hit Main Street, glancing at the clock. I had a ten-minute drive and thirty minutes until I needed to be there. Maybe I should drive around a little bit and kill time? Good lord, suddenly I'm a sixteen-year-old boy going on his first date.

"Geez, Dully, get a grip," I murmured to myself as I let off the accelerator and turned down a side street to kill time. "You're twenty-eight-years-old. This isn't your first rodeo."

I kept reminding myself of that over and over as I drove slowly through the darkened streets. It was the weekend before Thanksgiving, and we had an unusual burst of warm fall weather for the last few weeks. Soon the snow would fall and with the snow came football, fireplaces, and food. My mother would be sure to fill my fridge with lots of tasty, home-cooked Minnesota dishes to keep me fueled up.

I was tired of eating mom's food alone, though.

I'd rather be sharing it with someone I loved. I wasn't a bachelor by choice, I just hadn't found the right woman yet. I know a lot of women, and I always end up in the friend zone, if you know what I mean. Regardless of how many women I met, we always lacked the connection I yearned for. Until yesterday, when I was stuck in an elevator with a beautiful, white-haired angel. Yesterday I found that connection.

Snow is unique, like no woman I've ever met. Her easy-going conversation on the phone, when she had every right to be angry, told me the kind of person she was during a crisis. Her snow-white hair was stunning against her alabaster skin and her eyes were the color of a polished topaz. Her pink, plump, kissable lips rounded out the image of the natural beauty she was.

I did my best to hide my reaction when she introduced herself. I was sure she expected the usual smart-aleck comment when she told me her name. I didn't want to be like all the other guys, though. I wanted to be special, so even though her name surprised me, I didn't let it show. Honestly, she could have told me her name was Matilda, and it wouldn't have mattered. I was already hooked on Snow Daze.

I made a promise to myself a long time ago, and that was to wait for the right woman. I want the same kind of relationship my parents have, but I'm not naïve enough to think it doesn't take hard work and devotion every day to get it. It just seems to me if you find the right person, then the hard work is worth it. My parents have dealt with a lot of complicated situations in life with my siblings, but they always held each other close and supported each other through it. When I saw Snow in the elevator, well, I saw my future. I don't know a lot about her, but I'm determined to make it my job to show her nothing else matters but her.

I noticed the sign for Davenport Drive, and hung a left, pulling up in front of a new set of townhomes. I palmed the wheel into the parking lot, put it in park, and turned off the engine. I let out a breath. Okay, it's now or never. I unfolded myself from the car, grabbed the flowers, and shut the door with my foot.

I walked up the ramp, trailing my hand along the cold metal handrail to ground myself. Inside the door was a row of mailboxes. Above each box was a button. In the corner was a camera. I pushed the one that said *Snow* and resisted the urge to wave at the camera. There was a click from the door almost instantly, and I pulled it open. The hallway stretched before me and I meandered down it, trying to act casual and nonchalant. My heart was pounding when I reached unit five, and I wiped my palms on my pants legs.

I took a deep breath and rang the bell. A chain slid across the door on the inside, and the door opened. In front of me sat heart-stopping beauty.

"Good evening, Snow, would you care to join me for dinner?" I asked in my silliest English butler voice, hoping to relieve both our nervousness.

She laughed sweetly and motioned me in. "I will gladly join you for dinner, Jeeves. I've been looking forward to it all day." She paused and grimaced at the admittance, so I handed her the flowers to distract her.

"Beautiful white roses for my beautiful snowflake." I bowed slightly.

She blushed, the crimson red staining her cheeks in an adorable splash of natural color. "Thank you, Dully, they're beautiful."

She brought them to her nose, inhaling deeply. "Just let me put them in some water, and then we can go. Make yourself at home." She laid them on her lap and wheeled toward the kitchen.

I sat down carefully on the couch and smoothed my hands over my pants. It only took one glance around Snow's apartment to know the wheelchair wasn't just for research. The apartment was completely handicapped accessible. One glance at her tiny feet adorned with a pair of ballet slippers settled the question in my mind. They were not that of a grown woman, but that of a child.

I could hear her rustling around in the kitchen and I stood, checking out the pictures she had hung on one wall. They spanned the timeline of her life, and she wasn't standing in any of them. She was smiling in every single one of them, though, which in turn lifted my lips upward. There was rustling behind me and I turned, completely taken by the woman wheeling toward me wearing a smile that mirrored my own.

Snow

The white roses tipped with blue were gorgeous and fragrant as I readied them in a vase on the dining room table. I noticed him checking out the pictures I had on the wall, and tried to keep my breathing even. It's not a secret I told myself, he's probably already figured out you're in the chair permanently. I grabbed my jacket from the back of the couch, and he met me at the door.

"Ready to go?" I asked, struggling with the coat.

"More than ready." He smiled, and his green eye sparkled. "Can I help you with your coat?"

"That'd be great."

I handed it to him, and he held it so I could slip my arms in. Once I had it on, he held the door while I rolled out and locked it with my key fob.

"This place has some high-tech security going on," he said, as we headed for the front door.

"It's the reason I live here. A traditional peephole isn't useful to me, and one at my level is only going to tell me the color of the person's pants," I said, tongue in cheek, and he laughed as I hit the handicapped button for the door. "Instead, cameras tell us who is ringing the bell, and who is at the door. The key fob lets me lock, and unlock, the apartment easily, which is important when your hands are always busy. It's a nice system."

The air was brisk when we rolled out into the night. Yesterday's warm temperatures had given way to more typical Minnesota weather. "My van is over there." I pointed to the corner of the lot.

"It's a nice van, but I'm driving." He chirped the horn on the Dodge Magnum at the curb.

"Damn, you got style, boy." I whistled long and low.

He laughed, clicking the remote to raise the back hatch. "I'll admit I love driving this car, but it has a utility to it I use all the time, so it's as much a necessity as a toy."

I rolled my eyes sarcastically, but all in good fun. "Sure, you keep telling yourself that!" I said, laughing.

I rolled down the ramp to the passenger side door, and his chivalry kicked in. He opened it for me, holding the door open wide so I could pull the chair alongside it. I locked the wheels, unbuckled the seatbelt, and transferred onto the leather seat. I was extremely self-conscious when I lifted my legs in, but he didn't bat an eye.

"All ready?" he asked, and I nodded mutely, trying not to let the embarrassment show.

I reached over and clicked two buttons on the chair. Slowly, it started to fold by itself. Dully's eyes widened to the size of saucers, but to his credit, he just closed the door, picked up the chair, and stowed it in the hatch before sliding into the passenger seat. He belted himself in, then turned the car over, fixing the vents to let the heat pour in and warm us up.

My hand was on my lap, and he picked it up, holding it in his for a moment before he brought it to his lips and kissed it gently. The bottom dropped out of my stomach when he set it back on my lap and shifted into reverse. The flowers, his kind eyes, and the way he didn't ask questions I was afraid to answer. Those things told me the game was over and he'd won.

Gallo's was quiet by the time we arrived, so we took a booth in the far back. Dully held MAC while I transferred into the booth, which wasn't necessary, but seemed to be the equivalent to pulling out my chair for him. He tucked MAC around the back of the booth, near the coat rack, and rejoined me at the table. He busied himself with unwinding the scarf from around his neck and stowing his coat in the corner of the booth.

He was dressed sharply in a button-down shirt with the sleeves rolled to his elbows. The t-shirt underneath stretched across his chest, and I was acutely aware that even if he was barely a buck seventy-five, he was all muscle. It was suddenly incredibly warm in the restaurant when my mind wandered to what he'd look like without the shirt. I distracted myself by checking out his shoes and didn't bother to hide my giggle.

"How many pairs of those do you have?" I asked,

pointing at the grass green Crocs he wore, every hole filled with a letter of the alphabet. I noticed he had successfully spelled out *snow* on the left foot.

"A pair for every day of the week, baby," he answered seductively, just as the waiter arrived to take our order. I let him order the pizza and beer for us, while I asked myself again what I was doing here. *This is how Vincent sized mistakes happen, Snow*, I reminded myself. For some reason, myself didn't seem to care. For some reason, myself was enjoying itself and not interested in all the reasons why it shouldn't.

"That's some chair you got there," he said, motioning behind us while we waited for the waiter to return with our drinks.

"It's a new prototype, and yes, it's mine." The words came out of my mouth before I could stop them, and I sounded like an absolute idiot. *Smooth, Snow, very smooth.*

I was saved by the bell when the waiter returned and slid frosty cold beers across the table. I picked mine up and took a long pull of it, enjoying the coolness as it swirled toward my belly.

He took a sip of his and peeked at me around the mug, "Yes, it's your prototype, or yes, it's your chair?"

"Both?" I grimaced, and he chuckled. He set his mug down and leaned in over the table.

"Tell me about the chair first." He smiled openly and with interest in his eyes.

I blew out a breath and mimicked his posture.

"The chair is called MAC, or memory assisted chair. It's not super original, but it works for now."

"The chair has a memory? Like a computer chip or something?" he asked perplexed.

I leaned back and grabbed my key fob, hitting the button with the wheel on it. "Mac, forward, two clicks," I instructed in a loud, clear voice. The chair whirred, the wheels moved forward slowly, and it stopped after two rotations of the wheels. "Mac turn left then three clicks."

In two seconds, Mac was in front of me, and Dully's eyes were the size of saucers. "Mac, take a bow," I said, and the chair tipped forward twice.

"Show off!" Dully said, laughter filling his voice. I joined him, and it was a definite tension breaker.

"Mac, reverse, three clicks." I waited while the chair aligned itself. "Mac, reverse right, two clicks." The chair disappeared and I laid the key fob down and picked up my beer. "Demonstration over," I said artfully.

"I'm impressed. I had no idea that technology existed. You've programmed it to listen to your voice and follow simple commands?"

"That simplifies it down to brass tacks, but you're essentially correct. The idea behind Mac is to make certain tasks easier for the disabled. Say, for instance, you're out on a date, and you're strolling through the park or the mall. What's the one thing you'd like to do with your date?"

He paused and then picked up my hand, holding it in his. "Hold hands."

I forced my mind away from how warm his hand was wrapped around mine. "Exactly. I could say, *Mac, forward, hands*, and the chair would roll at a pace for walking and holding hands."

"That's a very cool application, Snow," he said sincerely.

"That's just the tip of the iceberg of what Mac can do. I'm designing him so handicapped mothers can carry their sleeping babies to their beds safely, the disabled can play sports easier, and so those of us in chairs have more freedom to live the way we want to. Speech recognition technology isn't new. It's been used for a lot of different applications. There are other people out there trying to do the same thing with wheelchairs, but they haven't had consistent success. We've found those bugs and worked them out. We still have a long way to go to make this available on the market. Yesterday, when I almost fell out of the chair?" I asked and he nodded, "that had been happening all day. It's two clicks forward and four clicks back in this business, just like anything else. I love it, though. Even on the days when Mac throws me onto the floor every few feet."

"Your passion comes through so powerfully when you talk about it. I'm truly impressed. I know you don't know, but I'm a special education teacher. Right off the top of my head, I can think of twenty different ways I could use that chair in the classroom."

I had done a little research. After all, that was my expertise, and I knew he was a special education teacher. I also knew exactly who he had gone to visit in the hospital yesterday.

"I'll admit I did a little research and discovered that you work for the local school district." He smiled, sipping his beer without judgment. "Did you spend the whole day at the hospital yesterday?"

He set his mug down, a pained expression on his face. "Is that lame? It sounds lame when you say it out loud."

I grasped his wrist gently. "I'm sorry, no, it's not lame. I didn't mean it like that. I just meant that's beyond the call of duty for a teacher to spend his entire day off at the hospital."

Oh, boy, I wasn't helping matters.

"Fair enough. Actually, I wasn't there as Adam's teacher, I was there as his friend. We didn't have school yesterday, so I had the whole day to spend with him. Whenever he's in the hospital, I stop in as much as I can, partly to relieve his mother, partly to keep him motivated to come back to school, and partly because I have a soft spot for Adam."

"That's a lot of partlys," I joked. "I think it's great that you invest so much time, and heart, into your students. I know that kind of devotion is rare nowadays."

He shrugged uncomfortably. "Some of my students need all of my time and heart. I've taught Adam for three years now, and he's had a rough go of it, but he always bounces back. He always comes back to my classroom happy as can be. The way I figure it, the least I can do is visit him in the hospital. It makes him happy, and that, in turn, makes me happy. It's really a win-win situation all the way around," he said winking. "But we weren't talking about me, we were talking about you."

"Oh, really?" I asked, trying to feign sarcasm, but he just nodded and sipped his beer.

"Let's see, where were we? Oh, yes, Mac. I've never seen a chair made of that material, that well-fitting, or one that folds that compactly without coming apart."

He was giving me an opening and I took it. "That's the other half of the research, fitting the chair to the end-user, instead of the other way around. All my old chairs were bulky and cumbersome, even the so-called lightweight ones. Mac is made to hug my curves, and get me where I need to go efficiently without excessive energy expenditures. Essentially, it's a motorized chair without the bulkiness of a large motor. There is a motor, but you wouldn't know it," I explained.

"Lucky Mac," he muttered, and I stopped short.

"Excuse me?"

He gave me a sly grin. "Mac gets to hug your curves."

I laughed and was about to make a smart-aleck remark when the pizza arrived at the table. Once again, saved by the bell.

His words rung in my ears, and the implications of them left me feeling like a schoolgirl. I definitely wanted to spend more time with Dully Alexander, even if the idea scared the crap out of me.

Chapter Four

I checked my phone for the tenth time in ten minutes. He texted me this morning to ask me on a *surprise* date. He wouldn't tell me where we were going, but I had agreed anyway, secretly excited about what he might have planned. But that was then, and this is now. Now, I'm nervous about what he might have planned.

Since our date at Gallo's last Sunday, I'd talked to Dully by text or phone every day. Wednesday and Friday, we met for coffee after school, and it stretched into dinner, and then dessert.

Over the last week, all of my fears and worries about getting involved with another man had mostly dissipated.

Our hours-long conversations had told me a lot about him. He was a typical Minnesota boy, playing football in the fall and hockey in the winter. After graduating from St. Mary's University, he moved back to his hometown to teach. He told me it never crossed his mind to go elsewhere. He loves Snowberry and the people in it.

He was extremely devoted to his students and spoke of them often and with high praise. His mom and dad live near the outskirts of Snowberry, and he has a large extended family all over the area. He usually spends at least a couple of weekends a month playing flag football or watching a game with his brothers. Not surprisingly, he loves his niece and nephew, and dotes on them, garnering him the *Best Uncle Ever* title.

I enjoyed spending time with him and listening to him talk about his childhood and his family. Not having any siblings, it was fun to hear the stories of the trouble they used to get into as kids. The way he told the stories made me yearn for that kind of family. A family I never had, and as much as I don't want to admit it, a family with him.

His soft, easy manner always lulled me into a sense of security and never made me nervous or self-conscious. Well, except for today. He told me we were going out, and I should wear something casual and comfortable. I was a little bit concerned but did as he said, and threw on my favorite pair of Adidas capris and a pink t-shirt to match.

I left the door open for him and curled up on the couch, hoping if he saw me relaxed and happy, he'd agree to stay in and watch a movie. I highly doubted it. He sounded like a man on a mission earlier, and I had a feeling I was in for an adventure.

I saw him enter the building on the camera, and hit the button for the door before he could ring it. In a matter of minutes, he was at my door.

"Come in, the door is open," I called from the couch.

He pushed it open and stopped in the entryway. "Well, hello, beautiful," he said, closing the door behind him and shrugging off his jacket.

"I didn't know your casual and comfortable would be that sexy." He sauntered over, joining me on the couch.

I glanced down at my clothes. "I didn't either?"

"Wow, sexy, and you don't even know it." I laughed softly and pretended to bat my eyelashes. "Oh no, don't be doing that. I won't be responsible for my actions if you keep that up."

His hand cupped my cheek, and I raised my eyes to his. The look in his was soft longing, and my breath hitched in my chest. "I won't hold you responsible," I whispered.

He sighed and lowered his lips to mine. His were soft and he kissed me gently, caressing my face with one hand while he kept the kiss close-lipped and tender. He pulled back, barely breaking the kiss before he kissed me again.

"What you do to me, Snow. You have no idea," he whispered.

I ran my finger down his smooth, soft cheek and let it come to rest on his chest. "Kiss me again," I ordered, surprising both of us.

He pulled me across him to rest on his lap and leaned down. He laid a kiss on each eyelid, and then on my lips while his hand stroked my back. I instinctively let my lips fall open, and he seized the opportunity, deepening the kiss and letting his tongue wander to mine. He let out a low moan when I kissed him back, fisting his shirt in my hand and tangling my tongue with his until we were both desperate for air. He pulled back, went back in twice more for short pecks, and then drew me to him tightly in a hug. He ran his free hand through my hair and blew out a breath.

"I'm sorry," he sighed, rubbing my back. "I got a little carried away."

"I wasn't complaining."

"I just don't want to screw this up, Snow," he confessed, running his finger down my cheek again. "I like you a lot, and I don't want to scare you or make you uncomfortable."

I glanced down at my hand still resting on his chest, and then back into the most honest set of unusual eyes I'd ever had the pleasure to gaze into. Everyone always said the eyes were the window to the soul, but I never believed it. Looking into his today, I no longer doubted it. His eyes showed me his soul, and I really liked what I saw.

"The only way you can screw this up is to walk away right now."

He pulled me into him again. "That's not happening," he whispered, kissing my forehead gently and wrapping both arms around me. "I have too many plans for today. Speaking of, we should probably get going."

"Where are we going?" I asked once he released me from his arms. I busied myself with running my hands through my hair to fix it. When I tried to scoot off his lap, he held me there without effort.

"Have you ever been roller skating?" he asked.

"Oh, all the time," I retorted, trying not to roll my eyes.

He smiled and tapped me on the nose with his finger. "Was that sarcasm?"

Yes.

"No, really, I go every weekend," I said while trying to hide my smile. He stood up in a flash with me in his arms. I grabbed him tightly around the neck, letting out a little yelp.

"It's okay, I got you," he assured me, leaning in and kissing me gently. A chaste peck on the lips that made me want so much more. He lowered me into Mac, and then knelt in front of me, buckling the belt before taking my hands. "Do you trust me?"

I nodded once. "I do. I just think you're going to be disappointed."

He held my hands and gave them a squeeze. "Never. As long as we're having fun, that's all that matters."

I took a deep breath, and that old saying about a first time for everything ran through my mind. "I'm ready to have some fun. What the hell, let's go roller skating!"

Dully

I pulled into the parking lot of the rink, still

reeling from that kiss on the couch. I tried to think of anything other than her warm body on my lap because my jeans were entirely too tight. Her soft curves rested in all the right places when I held her in my arms. I was quickly losing my grip on casual and slipping quickly into serious. Serious about her and serious about making her mine.

I put the car in park and shut it off, peeking at her from the corner of my eye. She stared at the building with two gigantic skater silhouettes on the wall, nervously shifting her eyes around.

"Hey," I whispered, and she snapped her head toward me sharply. Her blue eyes were scared, and I couldn't stop myself from leaning in and kissing her again. A light kiss I hoped would take away some of the fear. "Do you trust me?" I asked her, and she nodded mutely. "Okay, let me get Mac, and I'll teach you how to skate."

"I mean, Dully, this is weird. I'm in a wheelchair."

"Which already has wheels, so you're all set." I winked, and once she was smiling, I climbed from the car. Hidden by the back hatch, I did a fist pump. She trusts me. Now it was time to help her fall in love with me.

Snow

"Are you having fun?" he asked, setting a cold

soda in front of me and sliding into the opposite side of the booth.

"Honestly?" I asked, raising a brow. He nodded while sipping his soda. "I haven't had this much fun in years!"

His smile grew even wider if that was possible. We'd skated to slow songs and fast songs, raced a group of kids around the rink, and skated in the dark. He was an excellent skater and pushed me in Mac effortlessly around the rink.

"I'm glad, my falling snowflake. I love to roller skate. I guess it's the kid in me. If I can't be on the hockey rink, then this is the next best thing. Ask any of my colleagues, I'm the only one who actually skates when we come here on field trips."

I laughed, shaking my head. "For some reason, I don't even doubt it. You're a natural at it, that's for sure. Obviously, I couldn't skate as a kid. Being in a chair all my life, well, some would say it's just roller skating all day long, but it's not. This is …" I paused and gave him the palms up. "fun. When you push the chair and my hands are free, I feel like I'm skating just like everyone else. It's a lot like what I envisioned Mac would be for others, a little bit of freedom in an otherwise imprisoned world." I snapped my lips closed and twirled my cup on the table until he leaned in and stopped my fidgeting.

"Do you really want to feel freedom?" He raised a brow, and I leaned in to touch elbows.

"How free are we talking about?" I asked trepidatiously.

"No chair," he answered simply, and waited.

I let that roll through my mind but was pretty sure my face showed my confusion and apprehension.

"Do you trust me?" he asked for the third time that day.

"I do, but I can't skate, Dully."

We'd spent hours talking together, but I always avoided the subject of why I was in the chair.

He held up his finger before he jogged over to the DJ. They chatted for a moment, and when he returned, he leaned down into my ear. "I know you can't skate, but I can," he whispered as I gazed up at him.

"Dully, no, you can't carry me. I'm not little, really, don't let the chair fool you," I squeaked nervously.

"Sweetheart, I'm not worried." He slid one arm under my thighs, and the other around my back, swinging me up against his chest. I wound my arms around the back of his neck tightly. "Can you swing your legs around my waist?" he asked, and I shook my head to the negative, so he did it for me. He rested his hands under my butt, which was erotic even if it wasn't meant to be. I grasped the back of his neck and rested my head over his shoulder.

"I feel ridiculous, Dully," I insisted, just as the DJ's voice came over the speaker.

"This one goes out to Snow."

The lights went down, and *Fray* filled the rink with *Look After You*. Dully pushed off onto the smooth as glass floor and began to skate slowly, carrying me like I weighed nothing more than a small child. He skated slowly around the rink, sneaking kisses against my neck on the straightaways, and rubbing my back with one hand.

He made me feel safe, and for the first time in my life, I was free. Wrapped up in the arms of a man who didn't seem to care I spend my life trapped in a chair, I was free. I pulled back carefully and smiled, hoping it said everything I was feeling inside. He leaned forward and kissed me softly, letting his lips linger, but not taking anything more than the sweetness from mine. I leaned my head back on his shoulder, and he whispered in my ear. "Be my baby."

I know he couldn't hear me over the music, so I rubbed his back to the beat and hoped it told him what my words couldn't.

When the music faded, the DJ's voice filled the rink again. "Folks, I've been notified by the state police there's a bad snowstorm rolling in. It's gonna get nasty out there, so we will be closing down a little early to make it easier for those folks to do their job. Thanks for coming out today, and stay safe, my friends."

The lights came on and Dully skated me back to Mac, setting me down gently. "Did you know it was supposed to snow?" I asked, buckling my belt while he loosened his skate buckles and stowed them in his bag.

"I heard something about a snowstorm, but you know how it is around here."

"Wait five minutes and the weather will change!" I laughed aloud and he chucked my chin.

"Bingo."

We followed the stream of skaters out into what should have been two o'clock sunshine, but it was nearly dark already, the streets and cars obliterated by falling snow.

"Wow, okay, this is going to be a hefty storm. Crazy, it was almost sixty degrees yesterday. Stay here while I clean off the car. I don't want Mac to short circuit," he ordered.

He jogged out the door and I rolled out of the way of the other skaters to wait. I watched him wipe the snow off the back window of the car until he could get inside for the snow brush. I was rather enjoying watching his backside wiggle as he went around the vehicle brushing off the snow. He climbed in and started the car, probably turning the defrost up on high to fight the losing battle against the storm.

My mind was all a jumble as I sat watching him. It had only been a week since this man had found a way to make me forget a lot of things about my life. To him, I was just Snow, and nothing else mattered to him. It didn't matter that I was a doctor. It didn't matter that I was in a wheelchair. It didn't matter that a life with me would always mean more work for him. He didn't care because what I had to offer him outweighed my challenges. The idea scared me and invigorated me at the same time.

I watched him stomping off his feet and brushing off his coat, and I knew at that moment I probably loved him. *No probably about it, Chicka*, that little voice said. This time I laughed, instead of growled, at it. I was still laughing when he came back in and unlocked my belt. "Is it okay if I carry you to the car? I don't want you to get wet. It's coming down hard."

"Of course. I trust you," I said, unbuckling the belt so he could lift me from the chair.

He smiled and kissed my lips once before he backed up to the door and pushed it open with his very fine behind. He deposited me in the passenger seat and then went back for Mac. By the time he slid into the driver's seat, the windshield was covered in snow again.

"Got your belt on? I have a feeling this is going to be a tough drive."

His jaw was set with worry when he shifted into reverse. I'd lived in Minnesota my whole life, and I knew he was right. It was going to be a bumpy ride, so I said a silent prayer that we'd get home safely.

Dully

"Are you sure you don't mind?" I asked her for the tenth time since we arrived back at her place.

She was carrying a plate of cookies in one hand and milk in the other, with Mac doing the driving. "Dully, there were five cars in the ditch in the two miles it took us to get back here. No, I don't mind. In fact, I won't have it any other way," she insisted, setting the cookies and milk down on the coffee table.

Outside her window, a blizzard raged. When we pulled into her parking lot, it was already whiteout conditions. I wasn't sure I'd make it the ten miles to my house without going in a ditch or hitting another car.

On the bright side, I was staying with a beautiful woman, and she wouldn't have it any other way. I patted the couch next to me and she rolled over and climbed up, tucking her legs up behind her and grabbing a cookie from the tray.

"Should we watch a movie?" she asked.

"Sure, whatcha got?" I asked, leaning back and casually putting my arm around her shoulders.

She held up the remote and waggled her eyebrows at me. "Pay per view."

Chapter Five

Snow

After a marathon of Ironman, we decided dinner was in order. Since I never remember to grocery shop, all I had in the fridge was a loaf of bread, a dozen eggs, and a bottle of wine. He gathered it all and threw together a huge pile of French toast. We had polished it off, and I sat sipping wine while he washed the last few dishes. I tried to convince him to put them in the dishwasher, but he refused. It was amusing watching him try to wash dishes in a sink that barely came to his waist. I didn't mind, I could stare at his behind as he bent over the sink.

I had changed out of my skating clothes and into a pair of lounge pants and a warm sweatshirt. They were predicting over two feet of snow, and for the first snow of the season, that was practically unheard of. I was just praying by morning we'd still have power and heat. Living in Minnesota all my life, I was aware the chances were fifty-fifty of that happening. Dully leaned up against the sink and dried his hands.

"I think it's time for you to tell me the story," he said, a sparkle in his eye.

I cringed inwardly. Oh boy, here it comes.

"Snow Daze. How did your parents decide on it? Other than the obvious fact your hair is snow white." He smiled, pointing out the obvious.

Ah, okay, my name. That was a game I'd play.

"My hair has something to do with it actually," I began, handing him a glass of wine when he sat down across the table from me. "I was born in the Congo. My parents were missionaries at the time and had been there for years. When I was born, they saw my hair, which I had a ton of, and it reminded them of the first snow of a Minnesota winter. Now, most people roll their eyes when I tell this story, assuming my hair was blonde, but it wasn't, it was white as snow. I have pictures to prove it. Anyway, they named me Snow, clearly not thinking about the fact their last name was Daze. It was a constant trial growing up with the name Snow Daze."

He chuckled and nodded. "I thought I had it rough, but I have to agree, Snow is probably harder to explain than Dully. I like your name. It fits you. It really does."

"How did your parents come upon a name like Dully?" I asked curiously.

"It's simple, really, it's my mother's maiden name. Susanna Dully. It's a good strong English name," he finished, bowing like a butler again.

I laughed and shook my head at him. "I think she took one look in your eyes and knew straightaway you needed a name as unique as you are. Mom's have that way about them," I reminded him, setting my wine glass on the counter.

I had to step away from the wine, or I'd lose track of every good intention I had, especially when it came to Dully Alexander.

I was lying on the couch when he came out of the bathroom. It was after nine already, and the wine and good food had relaxed me after the events of the day. He lifted my legs by my pants, so he could sit before he settled them back on his lap.

"Let's play twenty questions. I'll go first." He grinned, and I nodded, waiting for the question. "Do you have any brothers or sisters?"

I swatted at him playfully. "You know this! No, I'm an only child. I lost my parents at an early age, and lived with my grandmother most of my life."

He took my hand, kissing it softly. "What's your favorite color?"

"Orange," I responded, and he raised a brow, but kept going.

"What's your favorite song?"

"Hakuna Matata."

That got a bark of laughter out of him.

"Have you ever been on a roller coaster?"

"Yes, at Valley Fair in 1996, first and last time ever."

"Why?"

"I barfed for two hours afterward. It wasn't

pretty." I made gagging sounds, and he slapped his hand over his mouth, trying not to laugh.

"Okay, moving on! Where did you go to high school?"

"McDonald-McMahan," I answered, and he whistled long and low.

"Whoa, that's a pretty high-end school."

"Well, I'm a pretty high-end lady," I said smartly, unable to resist laughing at the look on his face.

"What's your favorite food?"

"Gallo's pizza, hands down, but that French toast you just made was a pretty close second."

"Teacher's pet." He teased, tickling my belly. I was enjoying the lighthearted banter, but I knew eventually he'd ask the question that was heavy and dark. It was inevitable.

We played twenty questions for the next hour, going back and forth, thinking of new questions with each round.

There really wasn't anything I was afraid to ask him. He was very much an open book. I tried to be, but I was pretty sure my prologue still hadn't been read. I should tell him, it's just that he didn't much seem to care.

He had his hand resting on my shinbone for the last twenty minutes, and it was becoming uncomfortable. I shifted and tried to swing my legs enough that he'd move his arm, but being subtle wasn't working. He helped me straighten out and then moved back into the same position.

"Uh, Dully, could you, uh, could you move your

arm?" I asked in a rush, and he lifted it instantly as if he had burned me.

"I'm sorry, was I hurting you?" he asked, his voice laced with concern.

"Not really hurting me, no. After a little while, the pressure becomes uncomfortable." I shrugged nervously.

"Can you feel them?" he asked, and I gave him the so-so hand.

"I can feel pins and needles and pressure sensations, but I don't have the strength to use them. I don't feel light touch, hot or cold, either."

He reached down and tried to pull my slippers off, but I stopped him. "Please don't."

"I won't hurt you, Snow. You don't have to hide from me. Tell me your story. We all have one, and I want to hear yours." He kissed me then, letting his lips massage mine until they parted, and he slipped his tongue in to tangle with mine. When the kiss ended, he held my gaze while his thumbs caressed my cheeks. "Tell me, please. I hope you know by now I'm not going to walk out that door no matter what you tell me."

He was right, it was time to tell him. Something told me that in the end, it wouldn't matter. Our story had already been written, but he deserved to know the whole truth.

"I mentioned that I was born in the Congo?" He nodded, and I continued. "As you know, the Congo is relatively removed from modern society. At least it was twenty-eight years ago. My parents worked there as missionaries providing medical care for the villagers. When I was a few months old, I contracted polio and almost didn't make it. They brought me back to the States for treatment, but it was too late for my legs. I was never going to walk. I'm luckier than some people, though. My arms weren't affected and I can feel everything above my kneecaps."

He ran a finger down my cheek and paused with it against my lips, where I kissed it. "I won't say I'm sorry because I truly believe we all have a destiny in life. I believe the things that happen to us early on are what define us and shape us."

"I agree. No one ever let me feel sorry for myself. Instead, my parents encouraged me to be thankful for the abilities I still had. I was always frustrated with the lack of technology available in wheelchairs and mobility aids, though. After my dreams of being a ballet dancer fell through, I decided to set my course toward finding ways to change that."

He laughed softly, pulling my hand to his lips to kiss. "You know what I love about you? That you can be self-deprecating, and do it in a way that makes people feel at ease. That's not an easy task, I know. Did your parents contract polio, too?"

I shook my head. "No, they were vaccinated long before they went over there. They stayed in the States after my illness, and when I was about thirteen, they were offered an opportunity to go to Madagascar for a month. We lived with my grandmother, my mom's mom, and we both encouraged them to go and do what they loved to do. Their plane crashed in the ocean about twenty miles from the island."

"Oh, Snow, that's horrific. I wasn't expecting a plane crash."

"It was a hard time for my grandmother and me, but what gave us comfort was knowing they had gone off to help others. I knew in my heart if I hadn't gotten sick, they never would have stopped being missionaries, it was just who they were down deep in their souls. If I hadn't gotten sick—"

"No, my snowflake, you can't feel guilty about getting sick. They made the decision to bring a child into the world. They gave up the right to think only of themselves when they did that."

I patted his chest to calm him. "I don't feel guilty, Dully. My parents spent years here in Minnesota and around the United States, building churches, vaccinating the poor, and rebuilding communities after natural disasters. For some reason, it was just in their blood to help others around the globe, and I understand that now. My work is like theirs, just in a different way. I don't know where technology like Mac may someday change the course of a life, but I do know it will. That's all that really matters to me. I work hard to carry on the tradition of helping people the way my parents did, but in my own way."

"That's quite a story, Snow."

"I have to admit you're the first guy I've ever told the whole truth to."

"Really?" his brows went up, and I nodded. "I guess you do trust me."

"I do," I conceded, and he smiled.

He reached down and pulled the slipper off slowly. He massaged my tiny foot and then slipped his hand under my pants to caress my leg. "Dully, please, you don't have to do this," I whispered on a breath, fighting back tears.

He stilled his hand on my leg. "You know I spend my days with disabled kids, right?"

I nodded, searching his eyes for any indication he was going to leave. "I know, but there's something different about getting paid for it and, well, this," I whispered, motioning around us.

"Sweetheart, I can promise you right now that I don't do my job for the money. My guess is, you probably make three times what I do, at least. I do what I do because I love it. I spend my days with some of the greatest kids the good Lord ever put on this earth. They may do things differently, but that doesn't mean they can't do them. I learned that lesson a good long time ago, and it's served me well to never forget it."

I quirked a brow at him.

"Yeah, I have a story too, like I said, we all do. When I was ten, my brother, Jason, was born. My mother didn't even know she was pregnant with him until she was nearly five months along. He was born with spina bifida and has been in a chair his whole life. He's never let anything stop him, either. We played hockey, football, basketball, and went roller skating at that same rink for years. It never crossed either of our minds that he couldn't or shouldn't do whatever he wanted. Someday Mac might change his life, too. I don't really know what the future holds. All I know is that right now, holding you on my lap and feeling your soft skin under my fingers, is driving me crazy. I'll be straight with you, Snow, I've fallen hard for you. All of you. And this," he ran his hand over the sole of my foot, "doesn't change anything for me. You're a beautiful, funny, smart, caring woman. We have a connection I've searched for all my life. I may completely screw it up by telling you this, but I'm in love with you, Snow Daze," he whispered. He leaned in and feathered a kiss across my lips.

My brain was trying to process the information, but my heart was taking over before it could.

Dully's lips stilled over mine. "Stop. Don't think, just let your heart answer me," he begged.

I kissed him back with everything I had, hoping it said *I've fallen hard for you too, and I'm in love with you.*

He ended the kiss slowly and pulled back, gathering me to him. "You do all kinds of crazy things to me, Snow. If you only knew."

I did know because I could feel exactly what I was doing to him resting against my leg.

I rubbed my hand against his bulging zipper. "I might have an idea."

"Stop doing that," he hissed, and I moved my hand back to a safer spot on his chest.

"I feel like I'm in a romance novel," I murmured against his chest.

He leaned back and crooked one eyebrow at me. "Danielle Steel?"

I laughed softly into the quiet room. "Danielle Steel's new novel, Snow Daze." I gave him a cheeky grin.

"Oh, great title. Give me the synopsis," he said, running his hand up and down my leg.

"The heroine is stuck in a snowstorm with a handsome, sexy man as the wind howls outside the window. They're lying on the couch in front of the fireplace, stealing kisses and sharing their deepest secrets. You know what happens next."

He gave me the palms up. "Nope, I've never read a romance novel."

I hung my head, shaking it a little. Of course, he's never read a romance novel. He's a man, you idiot. How are you going to get yourself out of this one, *Miss Snow shouldn't drink so much wine*?

"Well, in most romance novels, the lights would go out about now, but I don't want that to happen, so we can skip that part. Then the handsome man would lift the heroine into his arms like she weighed nothing more than a feather, and carry her to the bedroom," I explained. Before I could take a breath, he was standing with me in his arms.

"Like this?" he asked, giving me an ever so slight lip tilt.

"Exactly like that," I admitted, a little breathless.

He carried me around the coffee table and down the short hallway to my bedroom, lowering me gently to the bed. He stood over me, his eyes filled with absolute lust. "What happens next?"

My face was beet red, but I decided to keep playing. "Next, the handsome man kisses her from head to toe. Unable to stop their raging passion, they make love all night until the storm subsides, inside and out."

"I think I like romance novels," he whispered. He stretched out alongside me and kissed my neck, keeping his weight off me with one knee, and caressing my breast through the thick sweatshirt I wore. I arched underneath him, and he took advantage of my bared neck, kissing it all the way to my collarbone and back again.

"I have a question." His words tickled my skin, and I sucked in a breath. "Can I write my own ending?"

I nodded because words failed me. He hung over me like a hawk, his eyes filled with lust and passion.

"Do you know what sounds good?" he asked, and I shook my head, afraid he was going to leave me lying here all hot and bothered while he made a snack. Instead, his hand snuck inside of my sweatshirt and rubbed a slow circle over my already aroused nipple. "A shower."

"Yes," I whispered on a moan.

He made quick work of removing my sweatshirt before he sucked my nipple into his mouth, right through the thin fabric of my bra. I writhed under him, moaning his name. When his eyes met mine again, they were clouded with lust. I struggled to get his shirt out of his pants, but he stilled my hands and grabbed the bottom, pulling it over his head.

His muscles flexed, and I sat up so I could run my hands over his warm skin, and through the light blond hair on his chest. He kissed me passionately while he stripped off my bra and let my breasts fall into his waiting palms. He kissed his way down to my now bare nipple and sucked it into his mouth.

"Dully, please, I need to touch you," I begged.

He released my nipple and stood before lifting me into his arms. "Not yet. I'm writing this story, remember?" he reminded me while he carried me to my bathroom.

He turned the water on and then lowered me to the bench of my dressing table. He flicked the button on his jeans, doing a slow striptease until he stood naked before me. He was at attention, and I reached out to run a nail up the side of him. He sucked in a breath and his eyes closed, a moan ripping from his throat. He stilled my hand and knelt, relieving me of the rest of my clothing until I was as naked as he was. Completely exposed in the light of the bathroom, I was self-conscious as he knelt in front of me, lust in his eyes.

"You're so beautiful, Snow. I want to make you mine."

"Please," I begged, and he picked me up, lowering me back down onto the built-in shower seat. He pulled the curtain closed, and I got a view of his backside. It was even better bare than in jeans. The water sprayed across my face and down my breasts to pool at my perfect triangle. He worked the soap into a lather and ran it over my breasts while he knelt in front of me. He leaned in for a kiss and I tentatively took him in my hand, the slickness of the soap and water creating friction that had him moaning against my lips.

"All's fair in love and war," he whispered against my lips. He slid two fingers inside me, and I gasped.

"I've never made love in a shower," I cried out, but he never broke rhythm.

"Good, I want to be your first and your last," he whispered lovingly, bringing me nearly to the brink of the cliff. I whimpered against his shoulder, begging him to let me go, but he wouldn't. I was still holding him in my hand and he backed off, slowing things down. He pulled his fingers from my heat and disengaged himself from my grasp.

"I want to be inside you, Snow. Right now," he ground out. "I don't have any protection, though."

I buried my fingers in his hair, and I kissed him with enough tongue to tell him I didn't care about protection.

"You don't need it. I'm on the pill."

The words weren't all the way out when he had lifted me up and sat, pulling me down over his thighs.

"Are you sure?" he asked, and I nodded. He lifted me and entered me slowly, holding me with his hands on my hips.

"Dully, please," I cried, begging him to take me. He let me sink the full length of him until he was buried all the way inside me. I braced my hands on his chest and let him set the rhythm with his hips. He sucked one nipple into his mouth, nipping at it and then tenderly circling it with his tongue until I threw my head back on a moan.

I had no control for the first time in my life, and I was high on the feeling. The passion and love I had for him overtook me and I couldn't stop the waves of ecstasy when they hit me one after another. I convulsed around him and he buried himself deep inside me and let go, moaning my name over and over.

When we could breathe again, he gathered me close to his chest.

"That was..." I laughed softly and buried my nose in his neck. "Mind-blowing."

He laid kisses along my neck and up to my ear. "That was just the first chapter. I plan to write this book for the rest of our lives."

Chapter Six

I sat in Mac and stared out the window of my apartment. It was Saturday afternoon, Christmas Eve. The big storm three weeks ago had changed my life in a way I had never seen coming. We'd spent every night together since. His apartment was an old colonial walk up, and since I can't walk up, he stays here. He offered to carry me up, and he did once, but frankly, it was too many stairs with me on his back. It didn't really matter much now, though. I'm not sure he has much left in his apartment. Most of his things had found their way here.

When we wake up tangled together in the morning, he spends the snooze button time kissing me before darting from my bed to get the first shower. When we aren't working, we're together, and it happened without a thought. It was natural, and in a matter of a month, I had lost my heart to him. There was nothing he wouldn't do for me, that much was obvious. Whether it was roller skating, shopping, snowball fights, or the annual Christmas light display, we had done it all, even when he had to carry me the whole time.

I glanced at the clock on the wall again. When he

left this morning, he told me there would be a delivery coming at three, and more directions would follow. To say I was perplexed was an understatement, but since I trusted him completely, I was anxious to see what it was.

The clock read two fifty-nine when a woman walked up to my mailbox and rang the bell after showing ID to the camera. I hit the button for the front door and swung Mac around to open mine. Her badge said Angelica's, and that made me smile. Angelica's was a dress shop on Main Street in Snowberry. It was family-owned, and on any given day, you could still visit with Angelica at the shop while she unwrapped and tagged new gowns, all at the ripe old age of eighty-five.

There was a knock, and I swung the door open to a smiling face, one I recognized now that there was no camera between us.

"Sarah!" I exclaimed happily, and she tried to wave around her heavy burden.

"Hi, Snow! It looks like I have an early Christmas present for you here."

I pulled the door open further so she could come in.

"Let's put it on my bed," I directed, leading the way. She relieved herself of her burden and handed me an envelope.

"I have strict orders that you follow those directions to a T," she instructed, patting me on the shoulder before letting herself out.

Oh boy. What is he up to now?

I wheeled to the bed and couldn't decide which to open first, the box or the envelope. I tapped my hand on my thigh for a moment just as my phone chirped.

"Did my package arrive?"

I typed back quickly. It *just got here, what should I open first?*

I waited while he typed, and laughed when the text came in. W*hat would Danielle Steel do? Love you, see you soon!*

I rolled my eyes and tucked my phone back into my pocket. As a woman, the answer was simple. Open the box! I locked Mac and opened the top of the box, parting the tissue paper to reveal a beautiful ice blue dress covered in sequins. I lifted it out and discovered it was sleeveless, with a matching half jacket for cover. It was breathtaking, and when the light hit the sequins, it glittered like falling snow-flakes.

Falling snowflakes.

I put the dress back in the box and shook my head a little, my eyes welling with tears. I was afraid to read the letter if the dress was already making me weepy, but I opened the envelope anyway.

"My Sweetest Snowflake,
I saw this dress in the window and knew you had to have it. It's what I see when I think of you because you have very quickly become the glitter and sparkle in my

life. I suppose you are wondering what to do now, right?

1. Put the dress on.

2. Put those cute white fur boots you have on with it.

3. Be ready at six. A white limo will pick you up. Bring Mac, we might need him. Don't be late.

Love you more ... Dully"

I laid the letter on the bed and wiped the tears from my eyes. Then I picked up the phone and called my own secret weapon.

Dully

I stood in the shop, nervously checking my watch. It was only three-thirty, but I had a thirty-minute drive back to Snowberry, and I still had to get ready. I walked through the store, gazing at all the beautiful diamonds as they sparkled back at me from under the glass. Even though I knew this was right, and Snow would love it, there was a little part of me that was afraid I was going to scare her away.

"She must be one special lady to be getting this for Christmas," the jeweler said as she broke into my thoughts. She pushed the box across to me, and I picked it up. After inspecting it one last time, I closed the box and handed it back to her.

"She's incredible, and that makes me the luckiest

man alive. I really appreciate the fact you got this done so quickly. I wasn't expecting you to be open today."

"You're our last customer. We're taking a well-deserved day off tomorrow. It's been a whirlwind holiday season, that's for sure." She smiled, holding out the now bagged box, which I accepted gratefully.

"And that is something every jeweler likes to hear." I laughed with her, shaking her hand. "I wish a very Merry Christmas to you and yours, Linda. Wish me luck."

I shook the bag, and she waved as I hit the door running.

The white limo might be a little much. I felt a little obnoxious sitting back here, staring out the window with no companion unless you count Mac. I hit the button to call the driver.

"Tom, where are we going again?" I asked for the third time, hoping he'd give me an answer.

"As I mentioned, twice, Dr. Daze, I will alert you when we arrive at our destination."

Well, wasn't that helpful? I settled back against the seat and wondered what was going on.

If he wanted to play mysterious, then I'd play hardball. Less than five minutes after I had called her, Savannah had shown up at my door. We had pulled my hair up into a bun and wound a ribbon into it to match the dress. Savannah did the *less is more* makeup routine, and I added my snowflake necklace and earrings to the ensemble. I was half expecting to end up at a ball, I was so done up, but something told me that was not what he had planned.

The car slowed and drew my attention back to the window. We pulled down a drive draped in blue icicle Christmas lights. Tom slowed the car at the turnabout and came to a stop in front of a pro-verbial winter wonderland. The door opened and I handed Mac out to Tom, who set him up on the com-pletely dry pavement and helped me into the chair. I buckled my belt and looked to him for answers.

"This is where I take my leave, and you will soon see why. Follow the path to the water's edge, and do your best not to cry."

He bowed, spun on his heel, and climbed back in-side the car.

Corny poetry or not, I was incredibly curious. The path was the width of my chair, and I followed it carefully, guided only by the blue lights that hung above and around me. I was wheeling down a path that led into the woods, and there were twinkling lights everywhere. In just a few feet, the path sloped, and in a few more feet, I found myself at the edge of a pond. Thankfully, it was a frozen pond. The scene that spread out before me was breathtaking, and now I knew why Tom mentioned the crying part.

The pond was shoveled clean of snow, and in the middle was a table for two, complete with candles, white and blue roses, a wine bucket, and lace tablecloth. The edges of the pond were adorned with solar lights, alternating white and blue, and sparkling against the snow. They gave the image of falling snowflakes.

"Wow," I whispered aloud, absolutely taken aback by the amount of effort that went into this night. Movement caught my eye, and skating toward me was a tuxedo-clad Dully, complete with a bowtie and blue pocket square. He took his time skating the length of the pond before shaving the ice as he came to a stop in front of me.

"Wow…" he breathed out, and that did seem to be the way we both felt. "Hello, beautiful, you are absolutely stunning." He knelt on the rug thrown over the snow, kissed me, and handed me a single white rose with blue-tipped edges. "Merry Christmas Eve, my beautiful snowflake."

I accepted the flower and took his hand. "I don't even know what to say. This is all so overwhelming."

"I wanted to make our first Christmas together special. I wanted it to be something you'd always remember."

"Well, you succeeded. I'm not likely to forget this before I die." I smiled with watery eyes, and he kissed me tenderly.

"Do you want to eat first or skate first?"

"Skate? In your arms?"

"I wouldn't have it any other way," he said huskily as music started to play.

He pulled me down the slight embankment in

Mac and then unbuckled the belt. "I think in this breathtaking, *make my heart stop and want to lay you down and make love to you* dress, you're going to have to ride sidesaddle, my lady."

He picked me up under my legs and settled me against his chest. I snugged my hand under his lapel and he took off skating to *Look After You.*

That was when I lost my battle with the tears.

I sat back against the chair and laid my napkin on the table. We had skated through several songs and then sat down for a traditional Christmas dinner of ham, Brussel sprouts, and Christmas pudding. His family's roots were deeply entrenched in the old English traditions, and when the tuxedo-clad waiter skated onto the ice, pushing a side table cart, there was no doubt in my mind it was Dully's brother. He disappeared as quickly as he came, and left us to enjoy dinner and each other's company.

Dully had set up a propane heater to keep us warm while we ate. "That's not going to melt the ice and send us sinking to the bottom of this pond, is it?" I asked, pointing to the heater.

He laughed, laying his napkin down and copying my posture. "No, it's only heating the air around us. It's going to take a lot more than that little bit of heat to melt this pond. Take my word for it."

"I'm going to go out on a limb here and guess this

is your parents' property?"

He nodded in the affirmative. "We grew up on this pond. I can't tell you the countless hours we spent skating and playing hockey in the winter, and fishing and catching frogs in the summer. I wanted you to experience a little bit of my childhood with me. Are you enjoying yourself?" He was sipping his wine, but I could tell he was nervous.

"I enjoy myself every day we're together, but this is one of those nights that will go down in history as the best night ever."

"Wow, and it's not even over yet," he said secretively.

I gave him the stink eye. "I'm not sure I can handle any more surprises. Oh! Do I get to meet your parents?"

I gazed at him expectantly, and he gave me the so-so hand. "Maybe later."

I cocked my head. "Obviously, they know about me, so why the secrecy?"

He wiped his hands on his thighs and stood, walking to me and kneeling by my chair. "Because I have one last thing to do."

"Okay, what do you have up your sleeve now? I think all that's left is dashing through the snow in a one-horse open sleigh," I sang.

He leaned in and kissed me long and hard, but his lips and hands were shaking the entire time. When the kiss ended, he kept hold of my hand in a vice grip.

"Snow, I know we only met a month ago, but I

also know we had an instant connection that day in the elevator. It was our meet-cute, and I couldn't get you off my mind. When I saw you again that night, something told me I had finally found the woman who completed me. You have filled the void I carried around in my heart. Your laughter is the best sound to fall asleep to, and your soft lips on mine are the best thing to wake up to. I told Santa there was only one thing I wanted for Christmas this year, and that was you. When you made room for my toothbrush, my wish came true."

I laughed softly then, squeezing his hand, which was still shaking. "That is a pretty big step, making room for the toothbrush. Forget about making room in the bed, once the toothbrush moves in, it's all over, you're getting hitched," I joked. My laughter cut off instantly, and my heart started to pound.

He was on his knee. His hands were shaking. He had gone to all this work to make the night special. Was this it?

"I was hoping you would say that." He let go of my hand and reached into his pocket, pulling out a box. He opened the lid, revealing a snowflake ring made of diamonds. "Snow, you've completed me. I know now that every experience I've had in my life was leading me to you. I'm the kind of man who follows my heart, and when I saw this ring, my heart said yes. Tonight, as I kneel here next to you, I promise to love you, kiss you, tease you, carry you, skate with you, and look after you for the rest of our lives. My beautiful snowflake, will you marry me?"

The ring glittered in the twinkling blue lights, and I wondered if I was actually in a romance novel. The man who knelt before me was so nervous but so genuine and honest about his feelings. He deserved the same from me, so I let a smile lift my lips upward as tears fell from my eyes. "I think you could teach Danielle Steel a thing or two about romance, Dully Alexander," I whispered. "I don't know why you're still holding that ring instead of putting it on my finger."

He cleared his throat and looked to the stars, tears glistening in his. "I didn't get an answer to my question."

I grasped his face in my hands and brought his lips to mine, kissing him with what I hoped was the right answer. When I pulled back, he wiped a tear off my face and smiled.

"Was that a yes?" he asked, taking the ring from the box.

"No," I said, and he glanced up sharply, "that was a yes, forever."

He did a fist pump and then slid the ring onto my finger. He leaned in for another kiss, and his family poured out onto the ice, but we were too lost in each other to notice.

Epilogue

One Year Later

I straightened the pictures on the mantel of the fireplace, letting my finger trace the length of the newest one. Dully was so handsome in a traditional English waistcoat on our wedding day, and the way he gazed at me that day, and every day since, made him even more handsome in my eyes. We had gotten married in June under the maple trees by the pond at his boyhood home, with his brother Jason as his best man, and Savannah as my matron of honor. Mac was decked out in white satin, and I wore a simple white sundress with blue ribbons to accent my eyes.

In the photo, we were sitting in the grass under the biggest tree, and it was meant to be one of those perfect wedding shots. The groom with his bride on his lap, her gown spread just so, while they gazed longingly into each other's eyes. I had winked at Dully and said, *here we are in that romance novel again,* and we both busted out laughing. He laid me down on the grass, kissing me as the photographer snapped the picture. It was my favorite picture of our day.

Dully had let his lease go on his apartment and

moved in with me January first. We were talking about buying a house, but the truth was, we couldn't find anything that would fit my needs. I was trying not to stress about it, but suddenly, I was desperate to find a bigger place. If we couldn't find one, then we were just going to have to build one. I twisted the ring on my finger nervously and spun Mac around to face the windows.

It was very early morning, Christmas morning, and the streetlights glowed against the quiet morning snow. The sun would rise soon, and we would go to his parents for their annual Christmas Day event. After his proposal last Christmas Eve, we had stayed with his parents and celebrated our engagement, and then Christmas, with them. It was a beautiful, relaxing day of getting to know them and getting to know Dully in a whole new way.

It turns out the limo driver, Tom, was actually his dad, Dr. Tom Alexander. The waiter was his brother, Bram, and his mom, Suzie, was responsible for the delicious meal. The proposal was a family affair, which they agreed to do without even meeting me first. They were, by far, the most welcoming family I had ever had the pleasure to know. His younger brothers, Bram and Jay, loved playing practical jokes and tried to make Mac run on their commands. It always left us all in stitches. His sister, Mandy, was reserved, but with two kids to look after as a single mom, she had earned that right.

His arms came around my middle, and he whispered in my ear, "Merry Christmas, Mrs. Alexander."

I twisted in my chair and kissed his lips. "Merry Christmas, Mr. Alexander."

He unbuckled my seatbelt and carried me to the couch, setting me down gently. "What are you doing up so early?"

"I couldn't sleep. Christmas excitement, I suppose."

"It's going to be an exciting day with my family. You know how it is. You're going to need your rest," he said, and I nodded.

"I know how it is. It's laughter, food, joy, carols, laughter, food, naps, and food," I said, chuckling.

He sat next to me and kissed me gently, pulling me onto his lap. "I got you a little something first."

"Oh, really?" I clapped my hands like a little kid, and he stood, going to the tree to take down an envelope.

Funny, I hadn't even noticed it up there. I guess my eye level and his eye level were two different things.

"Merry Christmas, Snow."

I raised a brow and took the envelope. "What's this?"

"Just open it!" he said nervously.

I flipped it over and pulled out the single sheet of paper, reading it aloud.

"Dear Dr. Fleetwood and Mr. Alexander,
I have reviewed the extensive research notes and videos you provided me regarding Dr. Alexander's memory assisted chair. I can say with absolute certainty this

prototype is like no other in conception. As President of Sunline Technology, I would take great pleasure in working with Dr. Alexander to bring M.A.C. to the mainstream market. This is a chair that will revolutionize the industry, and allow the end-user to live an independent, fulfilling life. Please pass along my congratulations to Dr. Alexander on the development of her fantastic technology, and let her know I will be in contact with her directly after the holidays.

 Respectfully Yours,
 Dr. Liam James"

I glanced up from the letter and into his hopeful eyes. "What…" I read the letter again and then dropped it to my lap. "I'm confused," I whispered.

He laid the letter on the table and took my hands. "I approached Dr. Fleetwood about submitting Mac to a few companies to help you get him on the market sooner. Dr. Fleetwood was adamant you wanted to work with Sunline because of their forward-thinking products and philanthropy for the disabled in all parts of the world. We know there are still a few glitches that need to be worked out, but that's what Sunline is about. They will help you take Mac to the next level, and get him on the market, where he belongs."

"Wow," I said on a breath. "I wasn't expecting this."

He ran a finger down my cheek nervously. "I know you weren't. I wanted to surprise you. Did I upset you instead?"

I gazed into his honest eyes and shook my head. "No, I'm not upset. I just wasn't ready to take this next step."

"I know you weren't because I know you that well, my snowflake. I also know you're a brilliant researcher, and what you have done with Mac is going to change the lives of so many people. I know you're scared, and that's what's holding you back, but this letter proves what I already know. You're ready. I wouldn't have done it if Dr. Fleetwood hadn't agreed with me. This is your time to show the world just who Dr. Snow Alexander really is."

I threw my arms around him and kissed his cheek. "I love you so much, Dully."

"I love you too, and I want you to be happy. This is just the beginning for you, and I couldn't be prouder to be standing by your side."

"Or carrying me?" I asked jokingly.

"Even better. Merry Christmas, sweetheart."

I leaned against his chest and looked out the window as the sun started to rise over the frosty morning. He had changed my life in so many ways over the last year, and now it was my turn to change his.

"Mac, forward, two clicks."

Mac engaged and stopped just short of the couch.

"Are you ready for your Christmas present?"

He nodded, rubbing his hands together. I grabbed a small envelope from under Mac and handed it to him.

He laughed zealously. "Great minds think alike, I guess?"

"I hope so."

He flipped it open, giving me a questioning eye before pulling the paper out of the envelope and scanning it quickly. He held it to his chest. "How did you do it?" His voice was hushed and surprised.

"I spoke with the couple who owns the lot on the other side of the pond. They're getting up in age and don't plan to build on that field now. They were thrilled to know the lot would be filled with the laughter of our children, and the extension of the family they love so much."

"I'm at a loss for words, Snow. We can build a house on that property?"

I took his hand in mine and held it to my chest. "I checked with the county, and it's a legal building site. We haven't had any luck finding a home, so I thought we could build one to fit my needs and the needs of our growing family."

He kissed me again, reminding me just why I married him. "We need to work on that part. Growing our family." He smiled against my lips, and I held up a finger. I grabbed a second envelope and handed it to him.

He stared at it in confusion and pointed to the return address. "This is from the hospital." He stared at me for a moment then flipped it over, pulling out the paper inside. "Snow Alexander, December twenty-fourth, HCG positive," he read, and I smiled softly when we made eye contact again. "What does that mean?"

"It's the start of the next chapter in our story, Dully. You're going to be a daddy. Merry Christmas, my love."

About The Author

Katie Mettner

Katie Mettner writes small-town romantic tales filled with epic love stories and happily-ever-afters. She proudly wears the title of, 'the only person to lose her leg after falling down the bunny hill,' and  loves decorating her prosthetic leg with the latest fashion trends. She lives in Northern Wisconsin with her own happily-ever-after and three mini-mes. Katie has a massive addiction to coffee and Twitter, and a lessening aversion to Pinterest — now that she's quit trying to make the things she pins.

A Note to My Readers

People with disabilities are just that—people. We are not 'differently abled' because of our disability. We all have different abilities and interests, and the fact that we may or may not have a physical or intellectual disability doesn't change that. The disabled community may have different needs, but we are productive members of society who also happen to be husbands, wives, moms, dads, sons, daughters, sisters, brothers, friends, and coworkers. People with disabilities are often disrespected and portrayed two different ways; as helpless or as heroically inspirational for doing simple, basic activities.

As a disabled author who writes disabled characters, my focus is to help people without disabilities understand the real-life disability issues we face like discrimination, limited accessibility, housing, employment opportunities, and lack of people first language. I want to change the way others see our community by writing strong characters who go after their dreams, and find their true love, without shying away from what it is like to be a person with a disability. Another way I can educate people without disabilities is to help them understand our terminology. We, as the disabled community, have worked to establish what we call People First Language. This isn't a case of being politically correct. Rather, it is a way to acknowledge and communicate with a person with a disability in a respectful way by eliminating generalizations, assumptions, and stereotypes.

As a person with disabilities, I appreciate when readers take the time to ask me what my preferred language is. Since so many have asked, I thought I would include a small sample of the people-first language we use in the disabled community. This language also applies when leaving reviews and talking about books that feature characters with disabilities. The most important thing to remember when you're talking to people with disabilities is that we are people first! If you ask us what our preferred terminology is regarding our disability, we will not only tell you, but be glad you asked! If you would like more information about people first language, you will find a disability resource guide on my website.

Instead of: He is handicapped.
Use: He is a person with a disability.

Instead of: She is differently abled.
Use: She is a person with a disability.

Instead of: He is mentally retarded.
Use: He has a developmental or intellectual disabil-

ity.

Instead of: She is wheelchair-bound.
Use: She uses a wheelchair.

Instead of: He is a cripple.
Use: He has a physical disability.

Instead of: She is a midget or dwarf.
Use: She is a person of short stature or a little person.

Instead of: He is deaf and mute.
Use: He is deaf or he has a hearing disability.

Instead of: She is a normal or healthy person.
Use: She is a person without a disability.

Instead of: That is handicapped parking.
Use: That is accessible parking.

Instead of: He has overcome his disability.
Use: He is successful and productive.

Instead of: She is suffering from vision loss.
Use: She is a person who is blind or visually disabled.

Instead of: He is brain damaged.
Use: He is a person with a traumatic brain injury.

The Snowberry Series

Snow Daze

Trapped in an elevator with a handsome stranger was the perfect meet-cute, but Dr. Snow Daze wasn't interested in being the heroine of any romance novel. A serious researcher at Providence Hospital in Snowberry, Minnesota, Snow doesn't have time for a personal life, which was exactly the way she liked it.

Dully Alexander hated elevators, until he was stuck in one with a beautiful snow angel. Intrigued by her gorgeous white hair, and her figure-hugging wheel-chair, he knows he'll do anything to be her hero.

When a good old-fashioned Minnesota blizzard traps them at her apartment, he takes advantage of the crackling fire, whispered secrets on the couch, and stolen kisses in the night. Dully will stop at nothing to convince Snow she deserves her own happily ever after.

December Kiss

It's nearly Christmas in Snowberry Minnesota, but Jay Alexander is feeling anything but jolly. Stuck in the middle of town square with a flat tire on his worn-out wheelchair leaves him feeling grinchy.

December Kiss has only been in Snowberry for a few months when she happens upon this broken-down boy next door. His sandy brown hair and quirky smile has her hoisting his wheelchair into the back of her four horse Cherokee.

When a December romance blooms, Jay wants to give December just one thing for Christmas, her brother. Will Jay get his December Kiss under the mistletoe Christmas Eve?

Noel's Hart

Noel Kiss is a successful businessman, but adrift in his personal life. After he reconnects with his twin sister, Noel realizes he's bored, lonely, and searching for a change. That change might be waiting for him in Snowberry, Minnesota.

Savannah Hart is known in Snowberry as 'the smile maker' in Snowberry, Minnesota. She has poured blood, sweat, and tears into her flower emporium and loves spreading cheer throughout the community. She uses those colorful petals to hide her secrets from the people of Snowberry, but there's one man who can see right through them.

On December twenty-fourth, life changes for both Noel and Savannah. He finds a reason for change, and she finds the answer to a prayer. Desperate for relief, Savannah accepts Noel's crazy proposal, telling herself it will be easy to say goodbye when the time comes, but she's fooling no one.

Noel has until Valentine's Day to convince Savannah his arms are the shelter she's been yearning for. If he can't, the only thing he'll be holding on February 14th is a broken heart.

April Melody

April Melody loved her job as bookkeeper and hostess of Kiss's Café in Snowberry, Minnesota. What she didn't love was having to hide who she was on the inside, because of what people saw on the outside. April may not be able to hear them, but she could read the lies on their lips.

Martin Crow owns Crow's Hair and Nails, an upscale salon in the middle of bustling Snowberry. Crow hid from the world in the tiny town, and focused on helping women find their inner goddess. What he wasn't expecting to find was one of Snowberry's goddesses standing outside his apartment door.

Drawn together by their love of music, April and Crow discover guilt and hatred will steal their future. Together they learn to let love and forgiveness be the melody and harmony in their hearts.

Liberty Belle

Main Street is bustling in Snowberry, Minnesota, and nobody knows that better than the owner of the iconic bakery, the Liberty Belle. Handed the key to her namesake at barely twenty-one, Liberty has worked day and night to keep her parents' legacy alive. Now, three years later, she's a hotter mess than the batch of pies baking in her industrial-sized oven.

Photographer Bram Alexander has had his viewfinder focused on the heart of one woman since returning to Snowberry. For the last three years she's kept him at arm's length, but all bets are off when he finds her injured and alone on the bakery floor.

Liberty found falling in love with Bram easy, but convincing her tattered heart to trust him was much harder. Armed with small town determination and a heart of gold, Bram shows Liberty frame-by-frame how learning to trust him is as easy as pie.

Wicked Winifred

Winifred Papadopoulos, Freddie to her few friends, has a reputation in Snowberry, Minnesota. Behind her back, and occasionally to her face, she's known as Wicked Winifred. Freddie uses her sharp tongue as a defense mechanism to keep people at bay. The truth is, her heart was broken beyond repair at sixteen, and she doesn't intend to get close to anyone ever again. She didn't foresee a two-minute conversation at speed dating as the catalyst to turn her life upside down.

Flynn Steele didn't like dating. He liked speed dating even less. When his business partner insisted, he reluctantly agreed, sure it would be a waste of time, until he met the Wicked Witch of the West. He might not like dating, but the woman behind the green makeup intrigued him.

A downed power pole sets off a series of events neither Flynn nor Winifred saw coming. Their masks off, and their hearts open, they have until Halloween to decide if the scars of the past will bring them together or tear them apart. Grab your broomstick and hang on tight. This is going to be a bumpy ride...

Nick S. Klaus

Nick S. Klaus is a patient man, but living next door to Mandy Alexander for five years has him running low this Christmas season. He wants nothing more than to make her his Mrs. Klaus, but she'd rather pretend he isn't real.

Mandy Alexander is a single mom and full-time teacher. She doesn't have time to date or for the entanglements it can cause. Even if she did have time, getting involved with her next-door neighbor, and co-worker, Nick S. Klaus, had disaster written all over it.

This Christmas, Nick's determined to teach Mandy that love doesn't have to be complicated, and he's got two of the cutest Christmas elves to help him get the job done. Will this be the year Santa finally gets his Mrs. Klaus under the mistletoe?

Other Books by Katie Mettner

The Fluffy Cupcake Series (2)

The Kontakt Series (2)

The Sugar Series (5)

The Northern Lights Series (4)

The Snowberry Series (7)

The Kupid's Cove Series (4)

The Magnificent Series (2)

The Bells Pass Series (5)

The Dalton Sibling Series (3)

The Raven Ranch Series (2)

The Butterfly Junction Series (2)

A Christmas at Gingerbread Falls

Someone in the Water (Paranormal)

White Sheets & Rosy Cheeks (Paranormal)

The Secrets Between Us

After Summer Ends (Lesbian Romance)

Finding Susan (Lesbian Romance)

Torched

Kupid's Cove

Don't miss the Kupid's Cove Series if you want to see more of Winifred and her friend, Kate Kupid!

Visit Me

Visit my website for all the news and updates regarding book releases and series! You can sign up for my once a month newsletter, which is always full of book information and newsletter exclusive giveaways! Plus, you'll find all my social media links in one place!

www.KatieMettner.com